Home for A While

By Lauren H. Kerstein

Illustrated by Natalia Moore

To all the children who have let me walk beside them for a while. May you always see your strengths. And to my mom, thank you for helping me see mine—LHK

For my parents, Liza and Darren. I cherish you both—NM

Magination Press

Books for Kids From the
American Psychological Association

maginationpress.org

Book design by Rachel Ross
Printed by Worzalla, Stevens Point, WI

Library of Congress Cataloging-in-Publication Data
Names: Kerstein, Lauren H., author. | Moore, Natalia, 1986- illustrator.
Title: Home for a while / by Lauren Kerstein ; illustrated by Natalia Moore.
Description: [Washington, D.C.]: Magination Press, an imprint of the American Psychological Association, [2021] | Summary: Calvin has lived in many houses that never felt like home, but Maggie, his new foster mother, helps him deal with his emotions when he misbehaves, and still offers hugs.
Identifiers: LCCN 2020028162 (print) | LCCN 2020028163 (ebook) | ISBN 9781433831874 (hardcover) | ISBN 9781433834769 (ebook)
Subjects: CYAC: Foster children—Fiction. | Belonging (Social psychology)—Fiction. | Home—Fiction. | Emotions—Fiction. | Behavior—Fiction.
Classification: LCC PZ8.1.K50974 Hom 2021 (print) | LCC PZ8.1.K50974 (ebook) | DDC [E]—dc23
LC record available at https://lccn.loc.gov/2020028162
LC ebook record available at https://lccn.loc.gov/2020028163
Manufactured in the United States of America
10 9 8 7 6 5 4 3 2 1

Calvin clunked his suitcase up
the steps of another house.

This isn't your home,

his thoughts shouted.

Nobody wants you,

his feelings rumbled.

"I'm so happy you're here,"
Maggie said.

"Sure." Calvin thumped his backpack onto the floor.

He wasn't ready to unpack yet.

That night, Maggie asked,
"May I hug you goodnight?"

"Nah," Calvin replied.

"Well then, sweet dreams,"
Maggie said.

Calvin lay in the dark.

Nobody wants you.

This isn't your home.

"Go away!" Calvin whispered.
He shoved his feelings down,
down, down, until...

Maggie told Calvin about his new school.
His fear exploded.

Bounce Bounce Bounce Bounce

He thought bouncing
a basketball would
quiet his feelings.

CRASH!

His hands shook
as he waited for
Maggie's reaction.

Maggie's forehead creased, but she didn't yell.

"Wanna shoot some hoops *outside*?" Maggie asked.

"Nah," said Calvin.

She waited, breathing in and breathing out.

Calvin's breath joined Maggie's.

His thoughts quieted as they walked outside.

He bounced the ball as high as the sky.

His stomach steadied like a spring breeze.

"May I hug you goodnight?" Maggie asked.

"Nah."

"Well then, sweet dreams."

"Maggie?" Calvin asked, his voice gruff.

"Yes?"

"Why do you want
to hug me, anyway?"

"I want to hug you because you're quite huggable."

"Oh, I am?"
"Yes, you are."

"Why didn't anyone else think that?

"Maybe they didn't realize you can bounce a ball for an hour. You're like a persistent beaver pounding sticks into his lodge."

"I am?"

"Like no one I've ever met."

The next morning, Calvin couldn't find his favorite shirt from Mama.

He thought throwing and kicking would quiet his feelings.

CRUMBLE!

His nightstand hit the wall and plaster showered the floor.

He wrung his hands, waiting for Maggie's reaction.

Maggie raised an eyebrow, but she didn't yell.

"Try this," she said, handing clay to Calvin.

"Nah." His heart pounded.

She waited, breathing in,
and breathing out.

Calvin's breath joined Maggie's. His thoughts quieted.

He squeezed, rolled, and kneaded the clay. He made snow people and snakes. Circles and spheres. His heart settled like butterfly wings.

"May I hug you goodnight?" Maggie asked.

"Nah."

Maggie blew a kiss. "Well then, sweet dreams."

"Why do you want to hug me, anyway?" Calvin blurted.

"Because you're quite huggable. You're like a strong superhero protecting the world."

"I am?"

"Like no one I've ever met."

Calvin imagined using superhero powers to control his thoughts and feelings.

Maggie wants me.

I like this house.

For homework, Calvin had to draw a family picture. Anger roared in his ears.

His fists curled.

His teeth clenched.

He thought jumping up and down would quiet his feelings.

CRACK!

The bed broke.

Calvin covered his eyes, waiting for Maggie's response.

Maggie crossed her arms, and frowned, but she didn't yell.

"Wanna take a walk?" she asked.

"Nah." Calvin's tummy twisted.

She waited, breathing in and breathing out.

Calvin's breath joined Maggie's.
His thoughts quieted.
He led Maggie outside.
Birds chirped.
Squirrels chattered.
Calvin's tummy settled like a quiet winter's snow.

Calvin breathed in and breathed out
as he finally unpacked his suitcase.

His eyes met Mama's.

He traced her hand-drawn
heart, and remembered
Maggie's words:

"You're quite huggable."

His body felt lighter.
Weightless.

"May I hug you goodnight?" Maggie asked.

"Why do you want to hug me, anyway?"

"Because you're quite huggable.
I love how you flip and fly
through the air. You're
like an eagle soaring
through the clouds."

"I am?"

"Like no one
I've ever met."

Calvin's tummy felt bubbly and warm.
He inched his hand toward Maggie's.

Maggie wants me.

This could be my home.

"Maggie, is this my home... for a while?"

"Yes Calvin, this is your home for a while."

He nodded.
"Could you hug me goodnight?"

Maggie reached out.
"You're like a cuddly bear cub."

Calvin melted into her arms.
"And you're like a mama bear."

"I am?"

"Like no one I've ever met."

An Author's Note on supporting the emotions
of children in temporary care is available at
bks.maginationpress.org/homeforawhile

Lauren H. Kerstein, LCSW, is a licensed clinical social worker who specializes in working with children, adolescents, adults, and families. She writes books for children and young adults and even wrote a textbook about Autism Spectrum Disorders. She lives in Englewood, CO.
Visit laurenkerstein.net
[f] @laurenkersteinauthor
[𝕏][◎] @LaurenKerstein

Natalia Moore has illustrated over 25 books and is also an art teacher. She lives in South Devon, UK.
Visit nataliamoore.co.uk
[f] @nataliamooreillustration
[𝕏] @NataliaMoore_
[◎] @nataliaillustrates

Magination Press is the children's book imprint of the American Psychological Association. APA works to advance psychology as a science and profession and as a means of promoting health and human welfare. Magination Press books reach young readers and their parents and caregivers to make navigating life's challenges a little easier. It's the combined power of psychology and literature that makes a Magination Press book special.
Visit maginationpress.org
[f][𝕏][◎][P] @MaginationPress